This book belongs to

....

Based on a true story . . .

Goose on the Farm
Copyright © 2013 by Laura Wall
All rights reserved. Printed in the United States of America

No part of this book may be used or reproduced in any manner whatsoever without
written permission except in the case of brief quotations embodied in critical articles
and reviews. For information address HarperCollins Children's Books, a division of
HarperCollins Publishers, 195 Broadway, New York, NY 10007.

www.harpercollinschildrens.com

ISBN 978-0-06-232439-9 (trade bdg.)

The artwork for this book was drawn with charcoal and finished digitally.

16 17 18 19 20   PC   10 9 8 7 6 5 4 3 2

❖

First U.S. edition, 2016

Originally published in the U.K. in 2013 by Award Publications Limited

Goose
ON THE FARM

by Laura Wall

HARPER
An Imprint of HarperCollinsPublishers

Today Sophie and Goose are
going on a school trip to the farm.

Mom helps Sophie make a packed lunch.

Then Sophie and Goose put on their boots

and wait for the bus with the other children.

There are lots of things to see on the way.

But Goose doesn't seem interested in the view.

Everyone is excited about
meeting the animals.

First they play with the bunny rabbits.

Next they feed the lambs.

And then they meet some fluffy chicks.

Goose starts to feel left out.

He wanders away to sit by himself.

But Goose is sitting on a nest of eggs,

and the mother hen chases him away.

Splash! Goose runs into a muddy puddle.

Now his feathers are covered in mud.

Goose sees a big fancy bird
with a funny feathery hat.

The peacock's colorful tail makes him jump . . .

Moo!

. . . and he bumps into a cow!

Goose isn't sure he likes the farm after all.

But wait. What's that?

A goat!

The goat smiles at Goose.

Goose follows the friendly goat.

They see a rooster crowing on a fence.

And they sing a silly song with him.

A turkey comes to say hello.

Baaaaa!

Honk!

And they all do a funny dance.

Then who should they see but Sophie.

"There you are, Goose!
I've been looking for you everywhere."

"Come on—it's time for lunch!"

The goat follows Goose and Sophie.

They wash their hands.

And they all sit down to eat.

But oh! There are no sandwiches!

Sophie's friend Ben kindly shares his lunch.

After they've eaten, the farmer takes the

children around the farm with his tractor.

And everyone has a pony ride.

Then they all play hide-and-seek.

But soon it's time to go home.

"What a lovely day!" says Sophie.

"Honk!" says Goose.